P9-BZE-294

THE
LITTLE RED HEN

By Patricia and Fredrick McKissack

Illustrated by Dennis Hockerman

Prepared under the direction of Robert Hillerich, Ph.D.

HARCOURT BRACE & COMPANY

Orlando   Atlanta   Austin   Boston   San Francisco   Chicago   Dallas   New York
Toronto   London

This edition is published by special arrangement with Childrens Press®.

Grateful acknowledgment is made to Childrens Press® for permission to reprint *The Little Red Hen* by Patricia and Fredrick McKissack, illustrated by Dennis Hockerman. Copyright © 1985 by Regensteiner Publishing Enterprises, Inc.

Printed in the United States of America

ISBN 0-15-302122-5

4 5 6 7 8 9 10   035   97 96 95

"Who will help me?" said the Little Red Hen.

3

"Oh, no. Not me."

So the Little Red Hen
did it by herself.

"Who will help me?" said
the Little Red Hen.

"No. I will not."
"No. No. I will not."
"No. No. No. I will not."

So the Little Red Hen
did it by herself.

"No. I cannot."
"No. No. I cannot."
"No. No. No. I cannot."

12

So the Little Red Hen
did it by herself.

"Who will help me?" said
the Little Red Hen.

"Not now."

"No. No. Not now."

"Not now. Not now."

So the Little Red Hen
did it by herself.

"Who will help me?" said
the Little Red Hen.

"I will, next time."
"Yes. Next time."
"Yes. Yes. Next time."

So the Little Red Hen
did it by herself.

"Who will help me now?"
said the Little Red Hen.

"I cannot help."

"I cannot help."

"I cannot help."

25

So the Little Red Hen
did it by herself.

"Who will help me?" said
the Little Red Hen.

"I will!"
"Yes. I will too."
"I want to help too."

But the Little Red Hen said, "No. No. No. You did not help me. I will eat by myself."